Dear Parent:
Your child's love of reading starts here!

Every child learns to read in a different way and at his or her own speed. Some go back and forth between reading levels and read favorite books again and again. Others read through each level in order. You can help your young reader improve and become more confident by encouraging his or her own interests and abilities. From books your child reads with you to the first books he or she reads alone, there are I Can Read Books for every stage of reading:

SHARED READING
Basic language, word repetition, and whimsical illustrations, ideal for sharing with your emergent reader

BEGINNING READING
Short sentences, familiar words, and simple concepts for children eager to read on their own

READING WITH HELP
Engaging stories, longer sentences, and language play for developing readers

READING ALONE
Complex plots, challenging vocabulary, and high-interest topics for the independent reader

ADVANCED READING
Short paragraphs, chapters, and exciting themes for the perfect bridge to chapter books

I Can Read Books have introduced children to the joy of reading since 1957. Featuring award-winning authors and illustrators and a fabulous cast of beloved characters, I Can Read Books set the standard for beginning readers.

A lifetime of discovery begins with the magical words "I Can Read!"

Visit www.icanread.com for information
on enriching your child's reading experience.

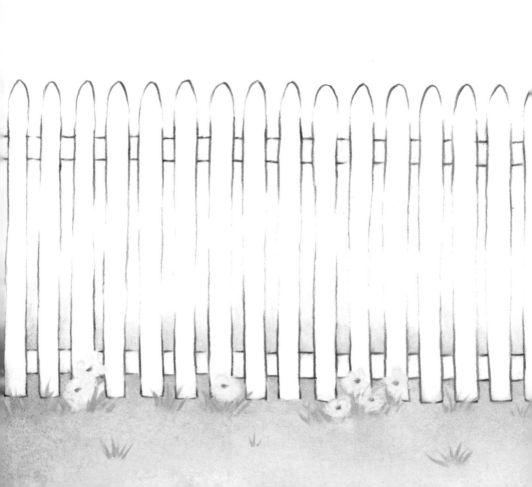

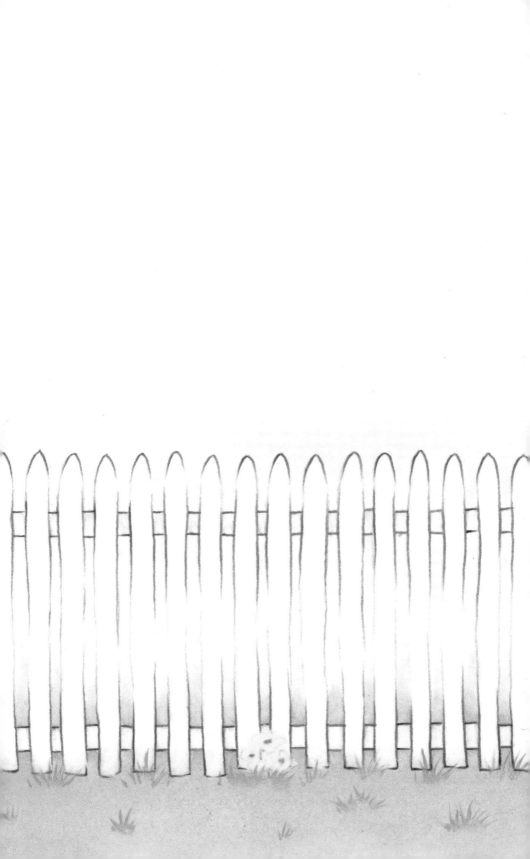

For Spencer
—L.M.S.

For Sophia
—S.K.H.

HarperCollins®, 📖®, and I Can Read Book® are trademarks of HarperCollins Publishers.

Library of Congress Cataloging-in-Publication Data
Schaefer, Lola M., date
  What's that, Mittens? / by Lola M. Schaefer ; pictures by Susan Kathleen Hartung. — 1st ed.
    p. cm. — (My first I can read book)
  Summary: When Mittens the kitten digs a hole under the fence in the yard, he meets a new friend—Max the dog.
  ISBN 978-0-06-054662-5 (trade bdg.) — ISBN 978-0-06-054663-2 (lib. bdg.) — ISBN 978-0-06-054664-9 (pbk.)
  [1. Cats—Fiction. 2. Animals—Infancy—Fiction. 3. Dogs—Fiction.] I. Hartung, Susan Kathleen, ill. II. Title. III. Title: What is that, Mittens?
PZ7.S33233Wha 2008   2007018374
[E]—dc22   CIP
                                                      AC

15 SCP 10 9 8 7 6 5 4
❖ First Edition

What's That, Mittens?

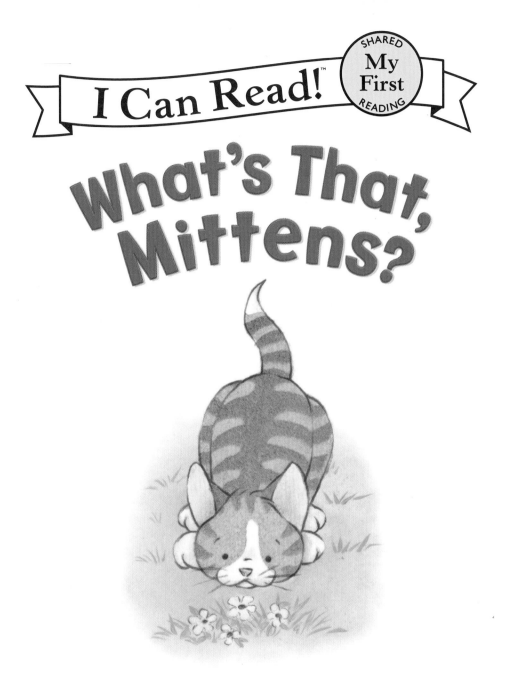

by **Lola M. Schaefer**
pictures by **Susan Kathleen Hartung**

HarperCollins*Publishers*

Mittens sits in the grass.

He is all alone.

He is looking for some fun.

Mittens hits his old ball.
Smack!

He smells a worm.

Sniff!

Mittens flips his tail

back and forth,

back and forth.

Then he hears,
Scratch! Scratch!

What's that, Mittens?
What's scratching
behind the fence?

Mittens runs to the fence.

He scratches in the dirt.
Scratch! Scratch!

Ruff! Ruff!

What's that, Mittens?
What's barking
behind the fence?

Mittens meows by the fence.
Meow! Meow!

Dig! Dig!

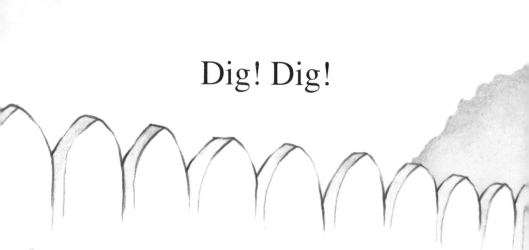

What's that, Mittens?
What's digging
behind the fence?

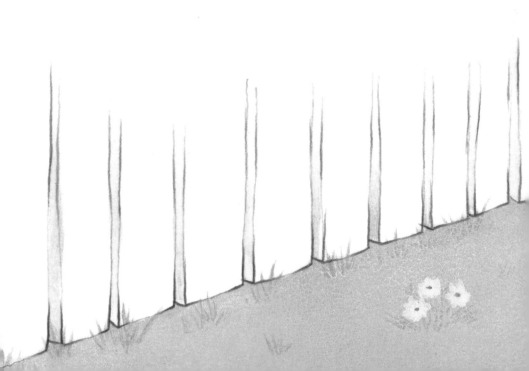

13

Mittens digs under the fence.
Dig! Dig!

Mittens digs fast.

Dig! Dig!

Mittens digs deep.

Dig! Dig!

Soon there is a big hole.

Mittens stops digging.

He looks under the fence.

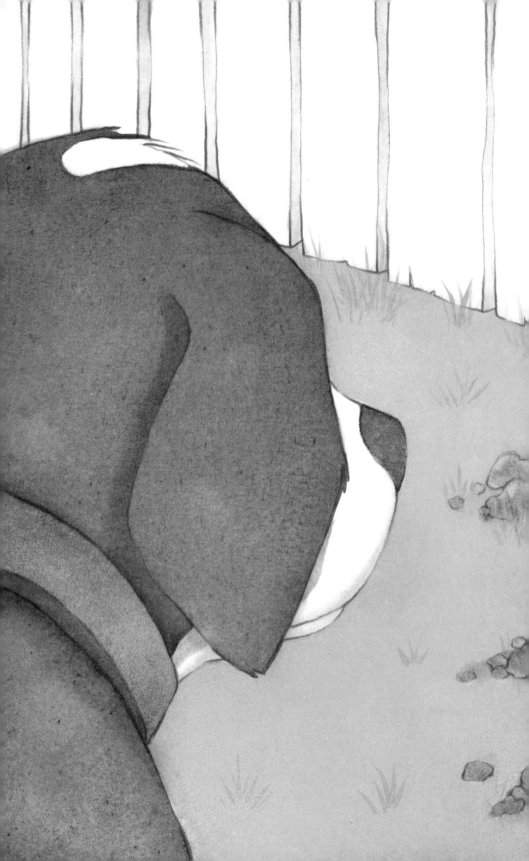

Mittens sees Max.

Face to face.

Eye to eye.

20

Nose to nose.

Sniff! Sniff!

Mittens likes Max.

Lick! Lick!

Max likes Mittens, too.

Mittens has found a friend!

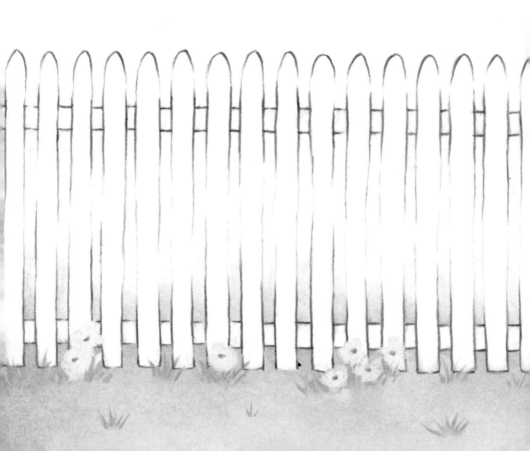

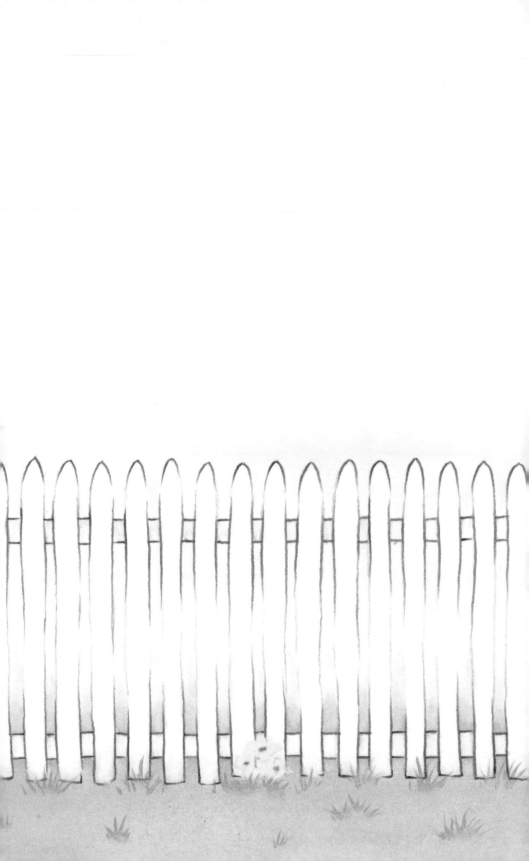